The Gospel According to Church Mice is one more example of how it is easier to swallow a tough and challenging topic like competition between denominations/fellowships when it's presented as a child-like fable. The genius of Dr. Ben Gray is revealed in the questions for discussion at the end of each chapter.

Rev. Janice Six
Associate Pastor
First Central Presbyterian Church
Abilene, Texas

"Get out the crackers because this parable will be food for mission-minded churches."

Rosemary Grigson Welch

United Methodist Pastor
Richmond, Virginia

In the words of Mary Poppins, "a spoon full of sugar helps the medicine go down!" Ben Gray has chosen a very palatable means of encouraging church people to swallow some very difficult truths about church. It would be difficult to read Dr. Gray's narrative and not identify yourself, your church and your own commitment to mission. Simple truth, like strange cheese, is sometimes hard to swallow, but once consumed, it inevitably produces healthy change.

Cindy Wiles, Director
Global Connection Partnership Network
Arlington, Texas

"With keen wit and philosophic insight Ben Gray has created a charming, modern parable sure to provoke discussion of the goals and practices of contemporary Christianity."

Dr. Ramon L. Delgado
Professor Emeritus, Montclair State University
former editor, Best Short Plays

the gospel according to

CHURCH MICE

the gospel according to

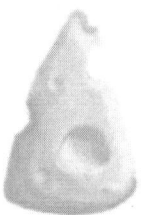

a church fable by Ben Gray, PhD

TATE PUBLISHING *& Enterprises*

The Gospel According to Church Mice
Copyright © 2008 by Ben Gray, PhD. All rights reserved.

This title is also available as a Tate Out Loud product. Visit www.tatepublishing.com for more information.

No part of this publication may be reproduced, stored in a retrieval system or transmitted in any way by any means, electronic, mechanical, photocopy, recording or otherwise without the prior permission of the author except as provided by USA copyright law.

This novel is a work of fiction. Names, descriptions, entities and incidents included in the story are products of the author's imagination. Any resemblance to actual persons, events and entities is entirely coincidental.

This book is designed to provide accurate and authoritative information with regard to the subject matter covered. This information is given with the understanding that neither the author nor Tate Publishing, LLC is engaged in rendering legal, professional advice. Since the details of your situation are fact dependent, you should additionally seek the services of a competent professional.

Published by Tate Publishing & Enterprises, LLC
127 E. Trade Center Terrace | Mustang, Oklahoma 73064 USA
1.888.361.9473 | www.tatepublishing.com

Tate Publishing is committed to excellence in the publishing industry. The company reflects the philosophy established by the founders, based on Psalm 68:11,
"The Lord gave the word and great was the company of those who published it."

Book design copyright © 2008 by Tate Publishing, LLC. All rights reserved.
Cover design by Stephanie Woloszyn
Interior design by Summer Floyd - Harvey

Published in the United States of America

ISBN: 978-1-60604-884-9
1. Performing Arts: Theater: General
2. Church & Ministry: Church Life: Evangelical
08.08.07

ACKNOWLEDGEMENTS

The "Gospel According to Church Mice" reflects the culmination of encouragement from family and special friends.

To my late mother, Pauline Gray, thank you for placing in my heart the desire to read.

To my father, Bennie Gray, thank you for providing constant, loving encouragement.

To my daughter, Bethany, thank you for believing in me.

To my loving wife, Louise, for being a constant source of prayer and support.

To my special friends who reviewed the fable and offered suggestions for improvement:

Dr. Eddie Sharp, Dr. Ramon Delgado, Dr. Larry Brunner, Nancy Haddox, and Rosemary Grigson Welch.

My special thanks to the leadership team at First Central Presbyterian Church, Abilene, Texas, for adapting the fable into a short play keynoting their missions week.

I am blessed beyond measure. My cup runneth over…

Ben Gray

CONTENTS

15   **Scene|1**
Welcome to Busyville

17   **Scene|2**
The Comfortable Church

21   **Scene|3**
The Church Across the Street

23   **Scene |4**
The New Church Down the Street

29   **Scene |5**
Looking for a New Church Home

31   **Scene |6**
A Visit to the New Church Down Town

33   **Scene |7**
A Return to the Comfortable Church

39   **Scene |8**
A Visit from Uncle Harry

43   **Scene |9**
A Meeting of the Big Cheese

53   **Scene |10**
Another Successful Meeting?

55	**Scene |11** *Going to the Edge of the Field*
57	**Scene |12** *Taking Cheese to the Middle of the Field*
61	**Scene| 13** *A Final Meeting of the Mouse Council*
65	**Scene |14** *The Case of the Missing Mouse*
69	**Scene |15** *The Final Chapter*
71	**Discussion Questions**

FOREWORD

Have you noticed the sign lately?

New and Exciting
Praise and Worship Service
8:30am Sunday

As attendance in local churches appears to gradually decrease, church leadership becomes concerned. Out of that concern, blue ribbon committees are formed to examine the problem of declining church attendance. After several months of meetings, committees present their awaited recommendation:

create a praise and worship hour. Sound familiar? These decisions sometimes result in fractionalizing a fellowship, causing a portion of its members to pursue membership elsewhere—only to learn that their "new fellowship" is experiencing the same dilemma—"What to do with music?"

Instead of taking the time and energy to examine the root issues of declining church membership, churches quickly resort to praise music as the "silver bullet" for its ailments.

As fellowships continue to struggle with their own version of "music wars" other ministries may temporarily "dropped off the radar screen." Has this happened in your fellowship? Is this happening with your fellowship now? If so, what goes unnoticed? Sadly, missions may be one of the first suffer from a misdirected focus.

How do we address this potentially divisive issue and at the same time create an opportunity for healthy dialogue? Historically, fables have created a viable means for a culture to explore difficult issues without alienating the audience. Consider the impact of John Bunyan's Christian classic fable, *Pilgrim's Progress,* upon the generation of its day.

The fable you are about to read is designed to provide congregations a non-threatening platform to discuss the needed shift from the style of music and becoming a missional church.

If one fellowship will benefit by moving its emphasis from "music to missions," I will consider this writing worth the effort. With God's help we can turn down the heat and turn up the light.

BEN GRAY

WELCOME TO BUSYVILLE

Narrator: Once upon a time, in a land far away, there lived a community of mice.

Some mice lived near the water. Some mice lived in the field. Some mice lived in a church. The people of Busyville made an agreement with the church mice. The mice could live safely in their church as long as the mice agreed to sweep the floors each day. In return, the people of Busyville would leave cheese in the church dining room at the end of the day for the mice to eat.

Ben Gray, P*h*D

There were three churches in Busyville—The Comfortable Church, The Church Across the Street, and The New Church Down the Street.

THE COMFORTABLE CHURCH

Narrator: This is a story of a family of church mice who attended The Comfortable Church in Busyville. Marty and Millie had two lovely children, Larry and Lilly.

Church mice who lived in The Comfortable Church followed special rules handed down from several generations of mice. No one is sure who wrote the rules. But one thing is sure—all the church mice from The Comfortable Church followed the rules. These rules were written inside their mouse pad.

Mouse Rule #1: Church mice must remain quiet at all times.

Mouse Rule #2: Church mice must only eat regular cheese.

Mouse Rule #3: Church mice must not show their teeth.

Marty and Millie's family lived comfortably near the Big Room in The Comfortable Church. Each morning the church mice family gathered to eat cheese.

As the family gathered for their daily meal, the children were very curious about the cheese. They wanted to know who brought the cheese. They wanted to know who put color in the cheese. But most of all, they wanted to know who made the cheese. Some of the answers were easy. Marty explained the cheese came from the kitchen located far away down the long hall. He also explained that he was the one who gathered the cheese in the middle of the night and brought it to the table for everyone to enjoy. One question, however, Marty could not answer,

Marty: Who makes the cheese? "What difference does it make? Cheese has always been in the kitchen. Has been and always will be. My family has round bellies—that's all I care about!"

Narrator: After working inside The Comfort-

able Church all day, the mice family quietly went to bed. That night Millie Mouse thought to herself
   Millie: Who does make the cheese?

THE CHURCH ACROSS THE STREET

Narrator: Sunday morning city mice began to gather at The Comfortable Church. As mice entered The Comfortable Church, Larry and Lilly noticed young mice playing outside at The Church Across the Street. That afternoon Larry and Lilly were curious why they were never able to play with the young mice from The Church Across the Street. Millie tried to explain. But the only thing she knew was that mice from different churches don't play with one another. That's the rule. Wanting to know more, they decided to ask father about the cheese eaters across the street.

Marty: This is all very complicated and even more difficult to understand.

Narrator: But the children were persistent in wanting to know more.

Marty: Well, if you must know our cheese is the same. It's just that we slice our cheese and they dice their cheese. Not only do they dice; they nibble their cheese.

Child Mice: Slicing and nibbling. Is that the difference? You mean we don't play with the mice from The Church Across the Street because we slice and they dice and nibble. That's hard to believe!

Marty: Nibbling is not good manners. Anybody can nibble, but not everyone can slice. Church mice who eat cheese have wonderful round full bellies and that's all that matters.

Narrator: That night Millie Mouse pondered these things.

THE NEW CHURCH DOWN THE STREET

Narrator: As Larry and Lilly grew older, they often wondered about the church mice who attended The New Church Down the Street. One Sunday morning Larry and Lilly Mouse could hear loud noises coming from The New Church Down the Street. For the past 10 years The Comfortable Church won the award for being the quietest church in town. It was no contest. They won the award "paws down." While Marty and Millie cherished "The Quiet

Church Award," Larry and Lilly wondered about the new church down the street.

One Sunday morning, Larry and Lilly asked permission to go down the street so they could hear the noise from The New Church Down the Street.

Marty: You want to leave The Comfortable Church and visit the rowdy church down the street? The noise will cause you to go deaf they are so loud.

Narrator: Still the young mice wanted to attend The New Church Down the Street.

Marty: Your mother and I have spent our lives helping build and clean The Comfortable Church and you want to go down there? We have everything you could possibly want right here. We've got great cheese, we've got the best cheese slicer, and best of all—we are quiet so you can think.

Narrator: Still the young mice remained curious.

Marty: No son or daughter of mine will go down there. Absolutely NOT!

Child Mice: Why not?

Marty: Because, I said so, that's why. Read my whiskers, No!

Child Mice: *(whining)* Please, pretty please…

Marty: Whine, whine, whine, all I hear is whine, would you like some cheese with your whine?

Child Mice: We don't want cheese, we want you to TELL us about their cheese.

Marty: If you MUST know, The Church Down the Street not only nibbles cheese, they serve cheese with flavor. That's what causes church mice to become so loud. I've heard that flavored cheese causes their church mice to kick their feet in the air and wiggle their whiskers. How undignified! Mice rolling on their backs, wiggling their whiskers and eating flavored cheese. My father and mother would roll over in their mouse pad if they knew our family ate flavored cheese. That New Church Down the Street is giving all church mice a bad name. What is Busyville coming to? End of discussion!

Narrator: That night Millie Mouse pondered these things.

Narrator: Next morning while the children were playing in the church, Millie gently reminded Marty that some day soon Larry and Lilly would grow older and would want to visit another church—maybe even becoming a church mouse somewhere else. This was too much for Marty to hear. He was restless all day. Marty and Mary decided to talk with their children before going to bed. Marty and Millie gently placed the covers around Larry and Lilly remembering all the wonderful times they enjoyed in The Comfortable Church.

Millie: Children, the time will come when you grow up that it will only be natural for you to want to visit The Church Across the Street that nibbles cheese. That's a safe place for you to go. I know some of the mice families over there. They're not just like us, but they're close. After much thought I've come to the conclusion that nibbling cheese might be all right, as long as you watch how much you nibble.

Child Mice: What about The Church Down the Street that serves flavored cheese, can we visit there?

Marty: You don't want to go there.

Child Mice: And why not?

Marty: Because (*pause*) because, there are too many mice at that church. No one will know who you are. You'll be treated like a number and not a mouse. Not only that, it's not safe down there. You might get hurt. They're adding walls, new rooms, new roof—there's just too much newness at The Church Down the Street. There's too much change. For the time being, you'll need to stay here and eat sliced cheese with us and be thankful you have a round belly!

Narrator: That night Millie Mouse pondered these things.

Narrator: As time passed, Larry and Lilly grew

older and wanted to decide for themselves where to eat cheese. But where? They could try to find another room in The Comfortable Church and eat the familiar sliced cheese. They could go to The Church Across the Street where mice nibbled cheese. Perhaps they could go to The Church Down the Street where mice ate flavored cheese. So many decisions to make. But decide they must. After eating much cheese and taking naps, Larry and Lilly decided it was time to discover for themselves where they belonged. They agreed to visit each church before making a decision about which family of church mice to join. It was a sad day. And yet it was a happy day for Larry, Lilly, Marty, and Millie. The Comfortable Church became even more quiet.

That night Millie Mouse pondered these things.

LOOKING FOR A NEW CHURCH HOME

Narrator: Larry and Lilly decided to visit The Church Across the Street because it was convenient. If things didn't work out they could always return to The Comfortable Church. Also, The Church Across the Street ate the same cheese. They learned that The Church Across the Street observed the same basic rules when they were growing up—remain quiet, eat together, and don't show your teeth. Members of the Church Across the Street had round bellies—just like their home church. The mice of this church wanted Larry and Lilly to know there was plenty of work to be done at this church. Since they came from a family of mice that had a long history of sweeping floors, they would be more than welcome to stay and eat cheese with them. Larry and Lilly accepted the invitation and decided to stay for a week.

Larry and Lilly liked The Church Across the Street, but they had always wondered about The New Church Down the Street. So, filled with cheese and curiosity, they quietly packed their bags and set off to visit The New Church Down the Street.

A VISIT TO THE NEW CHURCH DOWN THE STREET

Narrator: It was a long walk to The New Church Down the Street. They hoped all the walking would be worth the trouble of leaving The Comfortable Church and The Church Across the Street.

As Larry and Lilly approached The New Church Down the Street they began to notice something different. Young mice families were surrounding the door. After quietly walking in, they realized all the familiar rules were broken: the mice inside were not quiet, they showed their teeth, AND they served flavored cheese. While these changes would be too much for most families, Larry and Lilly stayed out of curiosity. Not only were the rules different, the mice looked different. Some mice had long shiney hair. Some mice had short whiskers. But all the mice wiggled their whiskers when they ate flavored cheese. The cheese tasted better than they had hoped.

While eating flavored cheese, Lilly noticed out of the corner of her eye a mouse standing with a crutch. It was Oscar, the mouse who injured his foot in a trap several months ago. Everybody thought Oscar had died. Not so. He was alive and a member of this church. Larry noticed the famous three blind mice were leading singing and showing their teeth. Blind mice eating flavored cheese! Everyone showing their teeth! This was all new to Larry and Lilly. This was the place to be!

That night Larry and Lilly pondered these things.

A RETURN TO THE COMFORTABLE CHURCH

Narrator: Larry and Lilly met other young church mice while members of the New Church Down the Street. They were married and had young mice of their own. After several months of sweeping at The New Church Down the Street, Larry and Lilly wanted to return to The Comfortable Church to visit Marty and Minnie to show them their new grandmice. So the young mice families packed their clothes and off they went to spend the weekend with Marty and Millie for a surprise visit. As they arrived at The Comfortable Church, everything was quiet. They gently knocked on the door. Very cautiously the door opened.

Child Mice: "Surprise! Surprise!"

Narrator: Marty and Millie were so excited to see their family again. It was good to come home.

The next morning all the family came to the table. But there was no cheese.

Child Mice: Where's the cheese? We're hungry?

Narrator: Millie Mouse explained that Marty had grown older and had trouble going down the long hall and bringing cheese to the table. As the younger mice moved on to other churches, the older mice in The Comfortable Church had to fend for themselves and worry about who will bring cheese to the table. After a few moments, grandmother tried to find the best of the situation. Her face lights up.

Millie: Are you ready for some good news?

Child Mice: Yes, grandmother, tell us the good news!

Millie: The good news is that for the eleventh year in a row we've won the annual 'Quietest Church Mice Award' in Busyville. It was a little disappointing, though.

Child Mice: How's that?

Millie: We were the ONLY mice present to receive the award. Usually, church mice from The Church Across the Street show up for the award, but they don't compete anymore—so we won the award paws down. Some folks think they're becoming louder than they used to be.

Marty: But not noisy as The New Church Down the Street. I don't think they will EVER win the "Quiet Church Award"—they grin and giggle too much!"

Well, your grandmother is not telling the whole story. I may not be able to get around like I used to, but I can still put cheese on the table. It's just that The Comfortable Church doesn't have near the amount of cheese that it used to. When your parents were children we had cheese galore. All the mice had round bellies. Now there are few mice. Hardly anybody has round bellies anymore. Now every crumb counts. Are you ready for the good news?

Child Mice: Tell us!

Marty: We still serve sliced cheese—Once sliced, always sliced. That's what we've always said.

Millie: We've been talking about ourselves too much. Tell us about The New Church Down the Street. We want to hear all about it.

Child Mice: The members are different from the Comfortable Church.

Millie: In what way?

Child Mice: Not only are our members young like us, but they look different. Most of our church mice have long shining hair rather than short hair. Our members show their teeth and nibble flavored cheese.

Do you remember the three blind mice that were members of the Comfortable Church when they were young?

Millie: Of course I remember them.

Child Mice: Now they're members of The New Church Down the Street and they sing a song about 'Once I was blind but now I see.' They are wonderful! Oh, do you remember the young smart mouse that grew up in The Comfortable Church—the one who answered all our questions? He's older now and people call him 'Double Click.' People ask him to help them with computers all the time. That's how smart he is."

Millie: I always wondered what happened to that smart mouse.

Child Mice: Do you remember Oscar, the mouse that got his leg caught in a trap a few months ago? He's alive. He walks with a limp, but he's OK. He's a member of our church. Things are different at The New Church Down the Street.

Since you don't have as much cheese as you used to, would you like to try some of ours?"

The Gospel According to Chruch Mice

Marty: I'm not so sure. Will it cause us to become noisy if we eat too much?

Child Mice: No, but it might cause you to grin!

Narrator: Marty tried flavored cheese. All the family watched carefully. Sure enough, Marty Mouse grinned slightly. Millie was happy that Marty tried the flavored cheese because she wanted to try flavored cheese for years. She tried a little flavored cheese and began to grin even wider than Marty! For the first time since their marriage, Marty and Mary saw each other's teeth! It was a sight to behold! Everyone was smiling. The quiet church wasn't quiet as before.

That night Millie Mouse pondered these things.

A VISIT FROM UNCLE HARRY

Narrator: Early the next morning, there was a loud knock at the door. Everyone could hear the noise—even the mice across the street. As Marty opened the door, there stood long lost Uncle Harry. All the children heard about Uncle Harry, but none had ever met the famous uncle. He looked just like his brother Marty Mouse except for one thing—Uncle Harry had a broad wide grin on his face. When Uncle Harry was young he would move around quite a bit. No one ever knew what happened to him. Some thought he had joined the circus and became friends with an elephant. But no one knew for sure.

What joy in the mousehold! Finally the family gets to meet Uncle Harry.

The grandmice began telling Uncle Harry about the cheese their grandparents had just eaten. Feeling a little embarassed, Marty and Millie confessed to eating a little flavored cheese.

Uncle Harry: See. A little flavor's not going to hurt you. I used to eat flavored cheese all the time. That's what caused me to start grinning. But to tell you the truth, flavored cheese is a thing of the past.

Marty: A thing of the past! How can it be a thing of the past if we never tried it? We still serve regular cheese.

Narrator: As they gathered around the table, Uncle Harry told the grandmice about other church mice he had met. He told them about all the wonderful types of cheese served in churches. Uncle Harry's stories had the grandmice sitting on the edge of their seats.

Child Mice: Tell us more about all the cheese you've seen.

Uncle Harry: Well, like I said, flavored cheese is almost a thing of the past. Now there are so many more types of cheese that church mice are eating.

Let's see...there's cheese with color. There's cheese with holes. There's cream cheese. There's cottage cheese. There's sharp cheese. Some mice even eat cheese with fish!

Marty: Cheese with fish! I don't want to even think about it! This sounds too strange!

Uncle Harry: In some places, mice are attracted to strange cheese because it is different. Sounds strange, doesn't it?

Marty: All this talk about strange cheese is too confusing.

Narrator: Uncle Harry told the Mouse family that he had spent less time with church mice and more time with field mice that lived in the pasture far away from the city. Uncle Harry explained that field mice had never seen cheese, much less eaten cheese. Only city church mice eat cheese.

Child Mice: No cheese? What do they eat?

Uncle Harry: Well, that's the problem. The field mice have very little to eat. They eat weeds. That's why they are so skinny. That's why I've come to visit Busyville. I'm trying to find a way to get cheese for the field mice. The cold winds are coming, and there will be no food for them to live through the winter. Did you know that more field mice die from hunger than from traps each year? It's true. We spend all of our time fearful of traps that people set for us, and we never think of the poor field mice. I don't know how to help the field mice. Maybe the church mice in Busyville can help. I'm a mouse that's trapped in my own thinking.

Child Mice: *(pleading)* We can help, we can help.

Uncle Harry: I'm sure you can. Maybe together with older mice we can make a plan. Will you help a brother?

Marty: I don't know what I can do. And I'm not sure what The Comfortable Church can do either.

Millie: Marty Mouse, I wish you would listen to yourself. Your brother asks for help, and you're not sure.

Marty: *(relenting)* We'll see.

Narrator: That night Marty and Millie Mouse talked.

Millie Mouse pondered these things.

A MEETING OF THE BIG CHEESE

Narrator: Since Marty Mouse was the oldest church mouse in Busyville, it only seemed fair for him to ask other church mice to come to the meeting. So, Marty went to each church and asked the church mice to come to a meeting to discuss what to do about the field mice.

The next day Marty Mouse introduced his long lost brother Harry to other church mice.

At first, the church mice politely listened to Uncle Harry. He told them about church mice from other cities.

Uncle Harry: Would you like to play a game?

Everybody: Yes, let's play a game! The name of the game is called 'Do You Know?'

Uncle Harry: "Do you know there are less young city mice than ever before?"

"Do you know there are fewer city mice joining churches today?"

"Do you know there are more field mice than city mice than ever before?"

"Do you know more church mice argue about which cheese they prefer rather than sharing their cheese?"

"Do you know most field mice have never heard of cheese, much less tasted cheese?"

"Do you know church mice have more cheese than they can possibly eat?

Narrator: The church mice were silent.

Mouse A: Excuse me, I don't mean to be stepping on your paws, but how do you account for so many church mice attending The New Church Down the Street if there are less city mice than ever before?

Uncle Harry: That's because young church mice are simply changing churches within the city. As older churches have less church mice, the newer churches are growing because they have younger mice. The number of city church mice, however, remain the same.

Narrator: This information came as a surprise to the church mice in Busyville. The city church mice were puzzled by Uncle Harry's news.

Uncle Harry: We are faced with a growing problem—how to remain quiet and grow at the same time. The greatest number of mice to be added to the city will come from the field.

Marty: All I know is that we have less young church mice to help us clean our floors than we did ten seasons ago. The older mice can't clean like we used to. If we don't get help cleaning the church like we agreed, we may not be able to live in the church anymore.

Mouse A: That's why we need field mice—to help us sweep our floors! We definitely need field mice in our church!

Mouse B: I'm not so sure having field mice in our churches is the answer. Field mice don't know how to work like we do. They just lay in the field, soak up the sun, and have fun all day! If they really wanted our cheese, they could find it. Besides, they may not fit in with church mice. As my pappa mouse always said, "You can take the mouse out of the field, but you can't take the field out of the mouse."

Narrator: All the church mice chuckled—except the mouse from The New Church Down the Street.

Uncle Harry: Maybe there's another reason we need to invite field mice to church.

Mouse B: And what might that be?

Uncle Harry: Rather than invite field mice to clean our floors, maybe we should invite them simply because they may not be able to live through the winter. Who knows? Some may want to stay after winter and help because they are thankful to be alive. *If there is no church, where can any of us go for shelter?*

Narrator: The church mice were silent.

Mouse B: What do you want from us?

Uncle Harry: I'm hoping *together* we can find a solution. Anyone have an idea?

Mouse B: Yes, let's ask people to solve our problem! Mice can't solve mice problems. People can solve our problems for us!

Uncle Harry: *(slowly)* I'm not so sure about people solving our problems.

Mouse B: Why not?

Uncle Harry: Once I saw people sitting in a concrete bowl, staring at green grass with white lines. They were WEARING cheese on their heads.

Everyone: You are kidding! People wearing cheese!

Uncle Harry: I saw it with my own eyes. I don't think you can trust folks who wear cheese instead of eat it.

Narrator: All the mice agreed.

Mouse B: Here's another idea. Let's trap the mice like people do!

Uncle Harry: We don't want mice to feel that they are trapped in church. We want them to *want* to stay and become church mice. Let's keep thinking. Are there any other ideas?

Mouse A: I've got it! I've got it! Let's have a contest! Church mice love contests.

Narrator: All the church mice agreed. A contest would be the best way to get field mice to become church mice. The church mice agreed to make signs inviting field mice to church. The signs would read "Come Eat Our Cheese." Each church could decide best how they wanted to make their sign. Uncle Harry was elected coordinator for the contest.

Marty: The field mice will love our sliced cheese.

Mouse B: It's not the cheese; it's how you serve the cheese that makes the difference.

Mouse A: *(boasting)* They'll love our cheese!

We'll win this contest. All the city mice joining our church prefer flavored cheese. Today's young mice are tired of sliced and diced cheese. They want something more exciting!"

Mouse B: I've eaten your flavored cheese, but it leaves me hungry. I want to go to a church where I feel that I've been fed.

Narrator: Arguing continued. Perhaps the contest wasn't such a great idea after all. Within a few minutes the church mice quit talking to one another. The silence was so thick you could slice it.

Uncle Harry: *(slowly)* Maybe this isn't about cheese. Maybe this is about something else. The more we argue about which cheese is best, the less time we have to share cheese with field mice. Winter is coming. Maybe we need to ask ourselves, not "Which cheese is best?" but rather, "Who's Going to Eat Our Cheese? Only church mice?"

Narrator: The church mice were silent.

Without a better plan, the mice agreed to proceed with the sign contest. The next day Uncle Harry visited each church to check on their progress. Most of the church mice were excited about the contest—especially winning.

After all the churches met, church mice at The Comfortable Church decided to not change their sign. Someone remembered that the sign was donated by a mouse family that died years ago. Members of The Comfortable Church were afraid that some of their members might get angry if the sign was replaced. So they decided not to change the sign but to sharpen the cheese cutter instead.

The Church Across the Street made a large colored sign that would dazzle your eyes.

The New Church Down the Street did something entirely different—they placed blinking lights around their sign. It was a sight to behold!

All the church mice were happy with their idea to attract field mice to their church. Each church was convinced they would win the "Come Eat The Cheese" contest

Sunday morning came. The church mice patiently waited. But no field mice came from the field.

Mouse B: See, we try to be nice and they don't come. Field mice want to stay in the field. You can lead mice to cheese but you can't make them eat!

Narrator: As the church mice continued arguing, suddenly there appeared a small number of field mice slowly walking down the street looking everywhere. Quickly, the church mice scurried to their doorways to welcome the field mice.

First, the field mice looked at the sign that hadn't changed. Then they looked very closely at the faces of the church mice at The Comfortable Church. They couldn't see the teeth of church mice. Slowly, the field mice walked by the church. Marty Mouse was shocked. Not one field mouse came inside to taste the cheese.

Marty: Hello, was it something I said? We've gone through the trouble of sharpening our cheese cutter, and they didn't come in. We've done all we can do. We are who we are. They are who they are.

Narrator: Next the field mice walked by The Church Across the Street and looked at the large colored sign in front of the church. Members of The Church Across the Street stood at the doorway showing their teeth. With caution, the field mice paused to taste the cheese, quickly nibbled, then returned to the street.

Mouse B: Can you believe that! We make a new colored sign and only a few field mice nibbled with us. We've done all that we can do. We are who we are. They are who they are.

Narrator: Finally, field mice walked to The New Church Down the Street. They couldn't help but see the large sign with blinking lights. Who could miss it? Church mice stood near the door and smiled. Field mice smiled back. Very cautiously the field mice came inside, nibbled the flavored cheese, sang a few songs, then scurried back to the field.

The Gospel According to Chruch Mice

Members of the Church Mouse Council gathered that evening and reflected on what happened that day.

Mouse A: Why don't more field mice come to our church? Maybe they just don't want to come.

Uncle Harry: Maybe you're right, maybe the field mice don't come to church because they are scared of the traffic in the city. Maybe it takes too much energy to walk from the field. Maybe they just don't know about the cheese. Maybe they don't know how good the cheese tastes. Maybe, maybe, maybe. I don't have the answers, but I DO know that winter is coming, and I'm willing to try anything to help the field mice.

Narrator: All the church mice agreed to meet the next day.

That night Millie Mouse pondered these things.

ANOTHER SUCCESSFUL MEETING?

Narrator: The next morning the Church Mouse Council met to discuss their first attempt to reach field mice.

Marty: It was a success as far as I'm concerned. We opened our doors—that's what's important—opening the doors.

Mouse A: It was a success as far as I'm concerned. We smiled, and that's what it's all about—smiles make the difference!

Mouse B: It was a success as far as I'm concerned, too. We fed more field mice than we've ever served before! Not to be bragging, but I think we won the contest.

Narrator: All the church mice were pleased with their efforts—all except Uncle Harry.

Uncle Harry: I wonder...how many field mice are there in the far pasture?

Mouse A: Hundreds, maybe thousands? Who knows! Why do you ask?

Uncle Harry: All I know is that winter is coming and more mice can live if they have cheese. The weeds will not be enough to live on during the winter. You're exactly right! Winter's coming and we need to be inside where it's warm.

Mouse B: *(growing impatient)* Yes, indeed! In fact, we're feeling a little breeze right now. It's time to go home and eat our cheese!

Narrator: The church mice agreed to return to their churches, eat cheese, and get together for another Church Mouse Council meeting the next day.

That night Millie Mouse pondered these things.

GOING TO THE EDGE OF THE FIELD

Narrator: A few days passed, and the Church Mouse Council met again to make a different plan. Uncle Harry was in charge. All the church mice listened. They were out of ideas.

Uncle Harry: Maybe we need a totally different approach. What if we take cheese TO the field mice?

Marty: Take cheese TO the field mice? None of us has ever done that before. I'm getting too old to haul cheese. I'm not as young as I used to be. It's hard enough dragging cheese down the hall much less trying to deliver cheese to the field.

Millie: Oh dear, you'll do just fine. It's not that far. You know how to bring my cheese each day. You can do it!

Narrator: Even though the other church mice had doubts about the plan, they agreed to take cheese to the edge of the field.

So off they went. Members of the Church Mice Council placed their favorite cheese near the tall grass and patiently waited and waited and waited. No field mice came to eat the cheese.

Mouse B: See, I told you. Field mice are field mice, and they'll never become church mice. They are who they are. We are who we are. If they're hungry they'll eat our cheese. They'll EVEN eat flavored cheese if they are hungry enough. Besides, we live in Busyville. It's time to go home. We've got much to do.

Narrator: As the church mice were making these comments, slowly dozens of field mice appeared from the tall grass and begin sniffing the cheese. To everyone's surprise, the mice ate ALL the cheese—-REGARDLESS of how it looked—-REGARDLESS of how it tasted. The Church Mouse Council returned to their churches to think about what they saw that day.

The church mice pondered these things.

TAKING CHEESE TO THE MIDDLE OF THE FIELD

Narrator: Early next morning, the Church Mouse Council met again to boast of their accomplishments. All their cheese was eaten. It was a great celebration for all the church mice!

Uncle Harry: What do you think would happen if we took our cheese to the *middle of the field* rather than to the *edge of the field?* I wonder if we could reach more field mice?

Marty: Maybe so, but I believe we've done

enough. We need to take care of the cheese for our church mice and quit worrying about field mice.

Uncle Harry: Maybe you're right. You know what I'm going to remember this winter?

Everybody: What?

Uncle Harry: I'm going to remember how much fun we had. I'm going to remember the field mice eating ALL our cheese. Won't that be fun to think about?

Everybody: Absolutely!

Uncle Harry: At the same time I'll be wondering how much MORE fun we could have had if we had taken cheese to the middle of the field. You know, it's not too late to find out.

Mouse B: Even if we agreed to take cheese to the middle of the field, no one has a map to show us how to get there. Suppose we get lost. Suppose cats find us. Suppose some of us don't come back.

Uncle Harry: I guess you're right. Let's all go home and have some cheese, cuddle up in our safe mouse pads, and sweep the floors.

Everybody: Sounds like a plan to me.

Marty: I agree with Harry. This is a matter of priority. We're in the middle of repairing our mouse pad. We can't do both. We can't repair our mouse pad and take more cheese to the middle of the field. Harry, you ask too much of us.

Uncle Harry: You're right. I guess it is a matter of priority. Would all of you agree to meet just one more time to make a final decision about taking cheese to the middle of the field?

Narrator: All the members of the Church Mouse Council agreed to meet one more time. Maybe this would be their final meeting.

A FINAL MEETING OF THE MOUSE COUNCIL?

Narrator: Next morning Uncle Harry was the first to arrive at the meeting. Then came other members of the Church Mouse Council—all except the mouse from The New Church Down the Street. Minutes passed. Still no mouse from the New Church Down the Street.

Church mice from The Comfortable Church came to the meeting because winter was coming and their church needed help sweeping floors. Church mice from The Church Across the Street came to the meeting because winter was coming and field mice needed shelter from the winter cold.

All the church mice were present except the mouse from The New Church Down the Street.

The church mice waited for the mouse from The New Church Down the Street to come to the meeting. They waited and waited. Still the church mouse from The New Church Down the Street didn't come to the meeting.

Marty: I'm not a bit surprised. They don't need to go to the field because they have plenty of church mice. They open the doors and city mice just flock in. They don't want to grow any larger. They are so busy feeding themselves flavored cheese and putting their legs in the air that they don't have time to take cheese to the field like we are doing. It's a matter of priorities!

Narrator: The Church Mouse Council made plans that evening to take cheese to the field mice in the middle of their field. Every detail was covered except how they were going to return safely to their church after being in the field. As they were leaving, Uncle Harry asked if any of the mice would go with him to visit the mouse from The New Church Down the Street and learn why he didn't come to the meeting.

Marty: What's the point? They've made up their mind. Why bother?

Narrator: After much discussion, members of the Church Mouse Council decided to go together to learn what happened to the missing mouse.

THE CASE OF THE MISSING MOUSE

Narrator: As they walked into The New Church Down the Street, they noticed sitting in a pew the missing member of the Church Mouse Council.

Uncle Harry: Did you forget about the meeting?

New Mouse: Not at all. I didn't forget. I was remembering what was said during the meetings of our Church Mouse Council. Someone made a comment about field mice being lazy and wouldn't be good members. What you didn't know is that once upon a time I was a field mouse. When winter came, our family tried to find food in the field, but there was none. Our mouse family went as far as we could go. I was the only mouse that made it to the edge of the field. That's when a city mouse found me and brought me to The New Church Down the Street. I've been warm ever since. I've forgotten about being hungry.

Marty: I'm sorry for the things I said. I didn't know you were a field mouse that became a church mouse.

New Mouse: That's okay. Perhaps I should have told you. Maybe I was ashamed for others to know about my being poor and hungry. Yet, I may have a solution about going to the middle of the field and not get lost.

Everyone: Let's hear it!

New Mouse: What if we were to leave small pieces of cheese on the trail as we traveled. When we get to the middle of the field we can leave the big pieces. Then we return to our churches by following our cheese trail. Not only could we find our way home, but other mice could follow us.

Narrator: The members of the Church Mouse Council were excited! Do you realize what might have happened if we hadn't taken the time to come here and learn what happened to this special mouse? Members of the Church Mouse Council were silent yet thankful for Uncle Harry insisting on bringing everyone along for the journey.

THE FINAL CHAPTER

The final chapter of this fable has not yet been written.

In fact, you are the one who writes the final chapter. It's not for me alone to write this ending.

Questions for your consideration...

1. What happened when church mice took cheese to the middle of the field?

2. What happened to The Comfortable Church?

3. What happened to The Church Across the Street?

4. What happened to The New Church Down the Street?

5. What did Millie Mouse finally say?

QUESTIONS FOR DISCUSSION BY CHAPTER

The Comfortable Church
Questions

1. What rules do the mice in your church have?
2. Do you take your cheese for granted?
3. Who brings cheese to your table?

The New Church Down the Street
Questions

1. Would your church win the award for being the "Quietest Church in Town?"

2. Can you describe the differences between your church and the one nearest you?

3. In what ways is your church like or unlike The Comfortable Church?

4. In what ways is your church like or unlike The Church Across the Street?

5. In what ways is your church like or unlike The New Church Down the Street?

6. Do the young mice in your church want to become members of other churches?

7. Do the mice from your church tend to exaggerate the features of another church?

A Visit to the New Church Down the Street
Questions

1. Have you ever thought about looking for a new church home?
2. If so, what are you looking for?
3. If not, what keeps you in your current fellowship?
4. What makes your church different from another church?
5. Can you explain the differences between your church and another church?

A Return to the Comfortable Church
Questions

1. When mice leave your church where are they going?
2. Do the mice in your church show their teeth?
3. Are you friendly to visiting mice?
4. How do you know?
5. Is the cheese different among churches in your city?
6. How are the mice different?

A Visit From Uncle Harry
Questions

1. What value do the "Uncle Harry's" bring to your fellowship?
2. How do you respond to the "Uncle Harry's" of the world?

The Gospel According to Chruch Mice

A Meeting of the Big Cheese
Questions

1. Is your church successful in getting field mice to taste your cheese?
2. In what way, if any, is your church reaching out to field mice?
3. Why do you think field mice don't come to your church?
4. Do you really want field mice to come to your church?
5. What gifts do field mice bring to your church?

Another Successful Meeting?
Questions

1. How do you think field mice would respond to your cheese?

2. How many field mice are there in your nearby field?

3. How effective are contests in reaching field mice?

Going to the Edge of the Field
Questions

1. What assumptions do the mice in your church make about hungry field mice?

2. What attempts have the mice in your church made to take cheese to the field?

Taking Cheese to the Middle of the Field
Questions

1. What kind of reasons would mice from your church give for not going to the middle of the field themselves?

2. Have you taken cheese to the edge of the field without going into the middle?

3. In what ways do you assist those who do take cheese to the middle of the field?

A Final Meeting of the Mouse Council?
Questions

1. Why do you think the mouse from The New Church Down the Street didn't come to this meeting?

2. What would you do about the mouse from The New Church Down the Street?

3. What assumptions do you make about churches that appear to be growing in numbers?